Alexander, Who's Not (*Do you hear me? I mean it!*) Going to Move

JUDITH VIORST

illustrated by
Robin Preiss Glasser
in the style of Ray Cruz

ALADDIN PAPERBACKS

The author and publisher gratefully acknowledge Ray Cruz,
not only as the talented artist who first brought Alexander
to life visually, but also for his contributions to the
initial development of art for this book, which, for
personal reasons, he could not complete. His spirit of
cooperation and his generous concern for the enjoyment of
young readers deserve the highest praise.

First Aladdin Paperback edition August 1998

Aladdin Paperbacks
An imprint of Simon & Schuster Children's Publishing Division
1230 Avenue of the Americas
New York, New York 10020

18 20 19

Library of Congress has catalogued the hardcover edition as follows:
Viorst, Judith
Alexander, who's not (do you hear me? I mean it!) going to move / Judith Viorst; illustrated by Robin Preiss Glasser.—1st ed.
p. cm.
Summary: Angry Alexander refuses to move away if it means having to leave his favorite friends and special places.
ISBN-13: 978-0-689-31958-7 (hc.)
ISBN-10: 0-689-31958-4 (hc.)
[1. Moving, Household—Fiction.] I. Preiss Glasser, Robin, ill. II. Title.
PZ7.V816A11 1995
[E]—dc20
95-5277
CIP AC
ISBN-13: 978-0-689-82089-2 (Aladdin pbk.)
ISBN-10: 0-689-82089-5 (Aladdin pbk.)
0810 SCP

For Miranda Rachel Viorst

—J.V.

For my sister Erica, who has always been there for me

—R.P.G.

They can't make me pack my baseball mitt or my I LOVE DINOSAURS
sweatshirt or my cowboy boots. They can't make me pack my ice skates,
my jeans with eight zippers, my compass, my radio or my stuffed pig.
My dad is packing. My mom is packing.
My brothers Nick and Anthony are packing.

I'm not packing. I'm not going to move.

My dad says we have to move to where his new job is. That job is a thousand miles away. My mom says we have to move to where our new house is. That house is a thousand miles away. Right next door to the new house there's a boy who is Anthony's age. Down the street there's a boy the same age as Nick.

There's no one next door or down the street or maybe for a thousand miles who is my age.

I'm not—DO YOU HEAR ME? I MEAN IT!—going to move.

I'll never have a best friend like Paul again. I'll never have a great sitter like Rachel again. I'll never have my soccer team or my car pool again. I'll never have kids who know me, except my brothers, and sometimes *they* don't want to know me.

I'm not packing. I'm not going to move.

Nick says I'm a fool and should get a brain transplant. Anthony says I'm being immature. My mom and my dad say that after a while I'll get used to living a thousand miles from everything.

Never. Not ever. No way. Uh uh. N. O.

I maybe could stay here
and live with the Baldwins.
They've got a dog.

I always wanted a dog.

I maybe could stay here and live with the Rooneys. They've got six girls. They always wanted one boy.

I maybe could stay here and live with Mr. and Mrs. Oberdorfer.
They always give great treats on Halloween.

I maybe could stay here
and live by myself in maybe
a tree house or maybe a
tent or maybe a cave.

Nick says I could live in the zoo with all the other animals.
Anthony says I'm being immature. My dad says I should take a last
look at all my special places.

I'm taking a look—but it won't be my last.

I looked at the Rooneys' roof, which I once climbed out on but then I couldn't climb back in, until the Fire Department came and helped me. I looked at Pearson's Drug Store, where they once said my mom had to pay them eighty dollars when I threw a ball in the air that I almost caught.

I looked at the lot next to Albert's house, where I once and for all learned to tell which was poison ivy.
I looked at my school, where even Ms. Knoop, the teacher I once spilled the goldfish bowl on, said she'd miss me.

I looked at my special places where a lot of different things
happened—not just different bad but different good.
Like winning that sack race.
Like finding that flashlight.
Like spitting farther than Jack three times in a row.

Like selling so much lemonade that my dad said I would probably have to pay taxes. My dad was just making jokes about paying taxes. I wish he was just making jokes about having to move.

I'm not—DO YOU HEAR ME? I MEAN IT!—going to move.

Nick says I am acting like a puke-face.
Anthony says I'm being immature.
My mom says to say a last good-bye to all my special people.

I'm saying good-bye—but it won't be my last.

I said good-bye to my friends, especially Paul, who is almost like having another brother, except he doesn't say puke-face or immature.

I said good-bye to my neighbors, especially Swoozie, who is almost like having a dog, except she's the Baldwins' dog instead of mine.

I said good-bye to Rachel, who taught me to stand on my head and whistle with two fingers, but she says don't try to do both at the same time. I said good-bye to Seymour the cleaners, who—even if it's gum wrappers or an old tooth—always saves me the stuff I leave in my pockets.

I said a lot of good-byes to a lot of people and got a lot of hugs and kisses, enough hugs and kisses to last for a person's whole life. I said a lot of good-byes—except I'm staying right here. I'm not going to move.

When the movers come to put my bedroom furniture on their truck, maybe I'll barricade my bedroom door. When my dad wants to tie my bicycle to the roof rack on top of the station wagon, maybe I'll lock up my bike and bury the key. When my mom says, "Finish packing up, it's time for us to get going," maybe she'll look around and she won't see me.

I know places to hide where they'd never find me.

Like behind the racks of clothes at Seymour the cleaners.
Like underneath the piano in Eddie's basement.
Like inside the pickle barrel at Friendly's Market.
Or maybe I could hide in the weeds in the lot next to Albert's house,
now that I know how to tell which is poison ivy.

I'd rather have poison ivy than have to move.

My dad says it might take a while but I'll find a new soccer team.
He says it might take a while but I'll find boys my age.

He also says that sometimes, when a person moves away, his father might need to let him get a dog to be his friend till he makes some people friends. I think that Swoozie Two would be a good name.

My mom says it might take a while but we'll find a great sitter. She says it might take a while but we'll find a cleaners who even saves gum wrappers and old teeth. She also says that sometimes, when a person moves away, his mother might let him call his best friend long-distance.
I already know the telephone number by heart.

Paul gave me a baseball cap. Rachel gave me a backpack that glows in the dark. Mr. and Mrs. Oberdorfer gave us treats to eat for a thousand miles. Nick says if I'm lonesome in my new room all by myself, he might let me sleep with him for a little while.

Anthony says that Nick is being mature.

My dad is packing. My mom is packing.
My brothers Nick and Anthony are packing.
I don't like it, but I'm packing too.

They better not try to move anymore
when we get where we're going to go.

Because this is the last time I'll do it.
The next time they won't make me do it.
Never. Not ever. No way. Uh uh. N. O.

I'm not—DO YOU HEAR ME? I MEAN IT!—going to move.